Relations Par Coeur

Compiled by

Gunwanti Harish Thanvi

Relations Par Coeur

COPYRIGHT
A UNIT OF UNITE PUBLICATION
Love.vibes143

DISCLAIMER

This anthology is a work of fiction. Our editors have tried their best to edit the content of all the co-authors and check the plagiarism. All the poems and quotes in this book are unique and are only published in this book.

ACKNOWLEDGEMENT

This anthology "Relations Par Coeur" comes out best with the support of endowment of growing writers and "Nikhil Sir". Compiling is really rewarding, I would like to thank all the co-authors of this anthology who trusted us and made this anthology possible with their beautifully penned write ups. I would like to thank "love.vibes143 publication a unit of Unite Publication" for helping me publish the anthology. And at last The Almighty, my mom and my friends, specially Shaurya Sharma, Rida Fatima and Himani Satpalkar, without whom i have never thought this.

ABOUT THE BOOK

Sometimes the relations which are formed by heart become more closer then those which are formed by blood. But in today's era where everyone is selfish it hard to make a bond with someone whether blood relation or not.But the one's who have a good bond with someone who is not in a blood relation but is related by heart are lucky.
As the relation's that are set by blood can be less effective than those set by heart. As the relation's by heart leave's an everlasting imprint.

INDEX

FOUNDER

Nikhil Jain

Compiler- Gunwanti Harish Thanvi

Co-authors
1. Seema Harish
2. Shaurya Sharma
3. Garima
4. Rida fatima
5. Himani Satpalkar
6. Pooja Gautam
7. R.V.Teena
8. Bhawna Mehta
9. Mohammad Yunus Akki
10. Sanskar Gupta
11. Shaheen Ansari
12. Kareena Verma
13. Naveen Bhardwaj
14. Krishna Motwani
15. Zainab Saboowala
16. Ami Patel
17. Mohammad Sohail
18. Esha Yadav
19. Pankaj Rajput
20. Agam Sachdeva
21. M.HARSHINI

22. Akash Chaurasiya
23. Trishna Chakraborty
24. Krishan Kant Sen
25. Saikumar Edunuri
26. Archishman Satpathy
27. A. K. Agrawal
28. Abdul Rahman (**रहमान बाँदवी**)
29. Komal Chauhan
30. Kajol Golchha
31. Beena shah
32. Jay Kailash Vyass
33. Richa Saini
34. Pragya Verma
35. Dhairya Manoj Thakkar
36. Parth Bipin Galia
37. Vanshika Parmar
38. Bandita Sahu
39. Anubhav Jha
40. Prerna Verma
41. Mohanapriya.K
42. Daniya Nadeem
43. Jasmine Panda
44. Ganesh Patil
45. Shubham Rathore
46. Radhika Sharma
47. HIDDEN DEMOISELLE
48. Khushi Arora
49. Diksha Motwani

Relations Par Coeur

50. Alfiya Suroor khan
51. Agarsana T K

FOUNDER
NIKHIL JAIN

Nikhil Jain is a writer from Dhule, Maharashtra. He is very fond of sharing his knowledge with others. He loves to do travelling, discovering new things and creativity. He likes to write, and he believes that by writing we can express our inner feelings very well. He has been the compiler of more than 30 books and has two online publications of his own named "Unité Publication" and "love.vibes143". To join them you can contact
Instagram : @love.vibes143
Email -love.vibes143@outlook.com

Compiler-
GUNWANTI HARISH THANVI

Gunwanti Harish is a SYJC student residing in Rajasthan. She loves to write which is the best way where she can express herself very well.

वो कुछ ऐसे हैं

वो कुछ ऐसे हैं,

जो मुझे अच्छे से जानते हैं,

जो मेरे दिल के सबसे करीब हैं..

वो कुछ ऐसे हैं,

जनिके बारे में लिखिते लिखिते

शब्द खत्म हो जाते हैं...

वो कुछ ऐसे हैं,

जनिसे आज तक मिलि नहीं,

मगर मिलिने को जी करता है...

वो कुछ ऐसे हैं,

जो बहन जैसे हैं,

दिल के बेहद करीब हैं...

वो कुछ ऐसे हैं,

जनिसे बात किए बनिा ,

मेरा दनि नकिलता नहीं हैं...

वो कुछ ऐसे हैं,

जो खुशयिों की वजह और होठों की मुसकान हैं,

मगर वो क्या जाने इन सब बातों को,

क्यूंकि रूठते तो वो भी हैं,

जब हम बात ना करे....

Love you....
Dedicated to- Shaurya Sharma, Rida Fatima, Himani

SEEMA HARISH

She is a housewife and a single mother of her two daughters. She had the passion to write from her childhood but due to some problems she left writing. But again she started it and expresses her feelings in them.

राह-ए-इंतज़ार

राह-ए-इंतज़ार में उम्र गुज़र गई,

ना वक़्त का पता चला ना खुद की खबर रही,

पहले लगता था, तूझे एक बार पा लूं,

होश तो अभी तक नहीं सम्भाला है,

पर तुझे पाने की अब बेताबी नहीं, चाह नहीं,

सांसो की अब श्रृंखला है,

एक छोड़ी तो दूसरी ली,

जीवन भी अब उसी भांति है,

पकड़ कर चलोगे तो जी ना सकोगे,

पसंद करोगे तो पकड़ना मजबूरी बन जाएगी,

प्रेम करोगे तो आज़ाद करना दिल की ख़्वाहिश बन जाएगी,

किसीसे मन मिल जाए यह तो मोहब्बत नहीं,

किसीके बिना मन ना लगे तो समझ लेना,

प्रेम प्रवाह होने लगा है,

झरना तेज़ी से समुन्द्र से मिलने लगा है,

पर तुझे पा लेते तो क़िस्सा खत्म हो जाता,

तूझे खोया है तो यकीनन कहानी लम्बी हो चली,

आशा की किरण थी अब वो भी खो चली,

नया उजाला जो भीतर चमका है,

हीरे की चमक भी उसके आगे फीकी हो चली,

खो कर अब जो पाया है,
खोने को कुछ रहा ही नहीं।।

तेरे साथ बिताए चंद लम्हे

रात बहुत बेचैन गुजरी,

खाली आसमान और सर्द सी पुरवाई थी,

कितनी ही अंगनित यादें साथ में तन्हाई थी,

आज रात फिर खोला था दिल के दरवाजे को,

लोग क्या जाने जनवरी में बरसात कैसे आई थी,

खामोश है चाँद,

बादल बिजलियां भी शान्त है,

फिर तेरी याद दिल पर घर बनाने आई थी,

अब तो आ ओगे,

नजर दूर तक फैलाई थी,

कब से रास्ता ताकती इस मोड़ पर आशा बन आई थी,

कोयल रात भर गाती रही डाल पर,

मेरे साथ शायद उसकी भी नींद भूल आई थी,

ले गए तुम प्रथम पंक्ति मेरे प्यार की,

आशा का अंतिम अंतरा गा रही शहनाई थी,

काश बचपन के सही भाव दे देता खुदा,

तेरे साथ बिताए चंद लम्हों के लिए सारी उम्र बेच दूं,

मन के एक कोने में यही भाव अंगणि भर आई थी।

SHAURYA SHARMA

"CA Student Embracing feelings through Words" Shaurya Sharma, she is residing in Punjab, Currently a CA final year student, passionate for writing, she is currently working as an Intern and a Project Manager with Spectrum of Thoughts Compiled Many books, coauthored 15+ anthologies still compiling! Bachelor of Commerce degree holder, Motivational Speaker, Novel writer, Story teller, Poet, Shayar, Singer, Meme Writer, Content Creator, Open Mic Participant, Inter Clear as per professional front, Intern/ Article Assistant in a Renowned Office ;Ashwani ; Associates; She is a bit bossy, sweet by nature and a bit sensitive to emotions, having leadership qualities always tries to warn people about the mistakes she did before, she follows a very simple rule: Be simple and amplify via simplicity; Writing since class 10th, got her first poem published in her school magazine, she is currently writing her own novel based on romantic fiction, launching by the end of the year, she loves writing, singing, dancing, painting, cooking as hobby.

Relations Par Coeur

Said a Doctor seeing her daughter waiting for her at home

Her curles were beautiful,
I tried to pat her head being willful,
Though it wasn't real but mild,
She still smiled like a child,
Through my phone's screen!

RELATION BY HEART NOT BY BLOOD

We don't share the same Womb,
But we share happiness and sorrows,
My online, I still hope to meet you soon!

GARIMA HARISH

She is not a writer, but only writes when she feels. She is MBA in HR and still studying. She is interested in doing new things. Even she loves art and craft and is even a teacher by profession.

दिल का रिश्ता

आँख खुलते ही तुम्हारी याद आजाना,

और फिर तुम्हारा फ़ोन न उठाना,

दिन की पहली खुशी और पहला गम,

दोनो साथ में बहुत ही कमल का लगता है,

यह एहसास न जाने क्यों होता है,

तुमसे कोई खून का रिश्ता तो नहीं है,

पर न जाने क्यों उससे भी बहुत क़रीब लगता है,

दिल से कुछ इस तरह जुड़े है हम दोनो,

की तुम्हारी एक पल की भी दूरी बहुत खलती है,

कुछ परेशानियाँ बनी रहे इसी तरह तो बेहतर है,

गुड्ड की तरह मीठे रिश्ते दिल से नहीं जुड़े होते,

और न ही वफ़ादार हो पाते है।।

FRIENDS

"Friends" Relations are from blood and some relations are from heart and some such relationships is friendship it's a kind of relations where the friend is like a sibling a sibling with another mother or. A brother or a sister without blood relation but a relation with heart.

RIDA FATIMA

Rida, Doctor by profession and writer by hobby. She is born and brought up in Rajasthan, and currently residing in U.P.

रिश्ते

कुछ रिश्ते दिल के बेहद करीब होते है,

ये रिश्ते दिल से जुड़े होते है

कुछ पराए अपने से लगते हैं

खुशियों में जो शामिल दिल से होते है,

रहमत रब की कहो या खुशनसीबी खुद की

ये दिल के रिश्ते नसीब वालो को ही मिलते है।

दिल से मिलवाया था

ठोकर खाई हमने,

सम्भाला भी अपनों ने था ,

रिश्तो में सबसे बड़ा खुदा था,

राह ताकते मुसाफिर को अपना बनाया था,

बेगानी इस दुनिया में,

कुछ रिश्तों को दिल से मिलवाया था।।

HIMANI SATPALKAR

Himani Satpalkar is a Financial Analyst residing at Mumbai, Maharashtra.

Who believes in, "मुझे जो अच्छा लगता है और जो मुझे मेहसूस होता है मैं वो कोरे कागज पे लखिती हूँ और पढने वाले उस लखिावट की शोभा बढा देते हैं।"

FRIENDSHIP

Two unknown person unknowingly comes under one roof, likes and dislikes aren't same of them. One is east another one is west. Without saying anything they recognize what other one is feeling. That's what we all call a true friendship.

ANIMAL AND A HUMAN BEING

One is human another one is animal but then too they are connected with heart. Humans some amount of food and share some love with him. He stay awake whole night just to check he is safe or not.

POOJA GAUTAM

Her name is Pooja Gautam. She is from Delhi. She has done Post-graduation in History and Bachelor in education too. She prefers to write about the awareness of women, or by raising vivid issues, put a questioning mark through her writing that where are the solutions to injustice and atrocities? She is fond of writing poems, shayaris, Ghazals, essays and articles and has also received many certificates in this field. Her interest lies in writing. She is highly liked by performing expressions in writing by words.

रिश्तों की एहमयित

कुछ रिश्ते बनावटी ही सही,

पर कुछ हक अपना जताते है,

अधूरेपन के ख़्वाबों में,

बनी असलियत से जो रूबरू कराते है,

जिन्हें सोचे ज़िन्दगी चली खून के रिश्तों से,

भी जो बड़े बन जाते हैं,

ऐसे अपनत्व की भावना से बने धागे,

दर धागे पिरोए जाते हैं।।

संबंध

करीबी लोग कभी दिखि नहीं,

दूरी मन भा जाए,

जो सुख दुख में साथ चले हैं,

वहीं ज़िन्दगी बन जाए है।।

R.V.TEENA

She is from Bikaner, Rajasthan
Completed her post graduation from mgsu, Bikaner.
Writing is her ambition and even her passion.
She likes to express her feelings in words which are not said to people.
She will love to be a part of anthologies and even her name in books,
In future she wants to see herself as an inspirable writer.

अनकही कहानी

हर बार हम सोचे वो हो जाए जरूरी नहीं,

हर रिश्ता हमसे जुड़ा रहे जरूरी नहीं,

कभी ख़्वाहिशें मारो अपनी तो,

कभी सपने टूटना ही होता है सही,

हर अपना अपना हो जरूरी नहीं,

कभी कभी कुछ परायों में भी छुपे होते है अपने,

कई साथ देंगे कहकर,

अक़्सर कुछ अपने छोड़ जाते है,

उदासी और निराशा में,

उम्मीद की किरण देने वाले फरिश्ते भी मिलते है कहीं।।

दिल के रिश्ते

पाया है मैंने भी कई अजनबियों को अपना होते,

शब्दो से दोस्ती के सफर में कई अनजानों को अपना होते,

कई बार हताश हुई हूं,

अपनी निजी जिंदगी से,

पर इस अजनबी सफर के रिश्तों को देखा है मैंने,

मुझको संभालते हुए,

यकीन कर पाना भी मुश्किल होता है,

जब हर अपना पराया हो जाता हैं,

रिश्ते मोहताज नहीं होते शब्दो के,

बस समझ पाना मुश्किल होता है,

ये जो नए साथी मिले है,

क्या कहूं इन्हे दोस्त ,प्यार,परिवार से बढ़कर माना है,

जिन्होंने शब्दो के धागे,

दिल के रिश्तों में तब्दील हो गए,

सच कहूं उम्मीद से बढकर साथ दिया है इन्होंने।।

BHAWNA MEHTA

Bhawna Mehta. She is presently pursuing B.Ed from Guru Jambheshwar University, Hisar. She like to pen down her thoughts. She has written two blogs and she won one Blog Competition also. She has interest in other activities also. She won District Level Debate competition and Dance Competition

एहसास

तुझे याद करतें हुए एक और रात गुजारी,

कुछ बातें थी,

जो तुझसे ना कह सकीं।

दिल को बहुत समझाया,

मगर धड़कन को ना रोक सकीं।

सब ने बहुत समझाया,

मगर में ना समझ सकीं।

ये तेरा प्यार नहीं,

मेरी आदत थीं,

जिसे में आज भी ना छोड़ सकीं।।

ख़्वाईश दिल की

सूरत क्या देखनी,

जब प्यार ही सरित से हो।

बात क्या करनी,

जब इशारे ही नजरों से हो।

दूर होकर,

जो पास हो।

खामोशी के पीछे के,

शोर को समझ सके।

काश कोई ऐसा भी हो।

बिना कहे मेरे अल्फ़ाज़ो को समझ सके,

काश कोई एहसास ऐसा भी हो।।

MOHAMMAD YUNUS AKKI

He is a businessman and did B.A. Loves to write, and is close to his family. Always believes everyone's time will come and they will get what they need.

MAA

Life began with waking up And loving my mother's face YES, we all start our day with our mother's smiling face. My day started when my mother gets me up early in the morning. For me, my mom is the best example of love and kindness in this universe. She knows how to take care of us. From the very tender age, I became a fan of her as I like my mom's hardworking and dedicated nature. My mom sacrificed a lot in order to shape my life. She has brought me up with utmost love and care. She could understand me even when I couldn't utter a word. Mother is another name of true love. A mother loves his child selflessly and doesn't expect or demand anything in return.

My mother whom I call mom turns our house into a home. My mother is the busiest person at our home. She gets up much before the sun rises and start to perform her duty. She cooks food for us, takes care of us, goes shopping and even plans our future too. In our family, my mother plans how to spend and how to save for the future. My mom was my first teacher. She also plays a vital role in shaping my moral character. She doesn't even forget to take care of our health. Whenever any one of our family members falls sick, my mother spends a sleepless night and sits beside him/her and take care of him/her for the whole night. My mom never tires of her responsibility. My father also depends on her whenever he finds any difficulty in taking any serious decision. The word mother is full of emotion and love. The value of this sweet word is truly felt by those children who don't have anyone to call 'mother'. So the one who has his/her mother beside them should feel proud. But in today's world, some wicked children consider their mother a burden when she gets old. The person who spends all her life for their children become a burden for their child at the last moment of her life.

Relations Par Coeur

Some selfish child even doesn't bother to send his/her mom to old age home.

This is really a shame and unfortunate incident as well. The government should keep an eye to those incidents and should take those shameless children in judicial custody. I want to stand with my mother like a shadow all the time. I know today I am here only because of her. So I want to serve my mother for the rest of my life. I also want to build my carrier so that my mom feels proud of me.

खून का रिश्ता

क्या नाम दे उन रिश्तों को,
जो दिल से जुड़े होते है,
खून से बढ़कर कई बार,
रिश्ता निभाया करते है,
होते तो खून के रिश्ते अहम है,
मगर जो दिल से जुड़े है,
वही अपनापन दिखाया करते है।।

SANSKAR GUPTA

Sanskar Gupta. Resides in Sitapur, Uttar Pradesh. Expresses his feelings by his pen. His thinking is, "Writing is only the thing in the world, where you can express yourself freely and entirely. He likes to inspire people through his writing skill."

चहकती सुबह

यह सुबह कुछ न कुछ कहती रहती है,

पानी की फुहार और मनमुग्ध फूलों की सुगन्ध,

ठंडी ठंडी हवाओं में बेख़्याली सी सबकी याद,

ये सुबह हमेशा अपनो के प्यार याद दिलाती है,

पर हमारी सुबह कॉलेज जाने के लिए ही होती है,

शायद रात कॉपी- कितिाब में बितिाने के लिए होती है।।

इक तमन्ना

शायद तकदीर नहीं ये,

तमन्ना है मेरी,

ख़्वाबों में मुमकिन पर,

शायद मुमकिन नहीं,

इक दफा सो लूं लिपटकर,

उसकी जुल्फ़ों में,

उन्हीं खुशबत जुल्फ़ों में,

उसको जी लूं ज़िंदगी में।।

इतिहास

हम सुरक्षित हैं जब वो खुद को असुरक्षित करते हैं,

अपना घर खुशियां सबसे खुद को मोहताज़ करते हैं

देश और हमारे लिए वो खुद ही मिट जाया करते हैं,

हर तख़्ती से मिटा खुद को इतिहास में दर्ज करते हैं।।

यादें

हमारी यादें ये हमेशा साथ रहेंगी,

दोस्ताना है ये हमारा, सबके साथ रहेगा,

जब भी मुड़कर इन यादों पर आऊंगा,

सिर्फ दोस्तों की ही फ़रियाद करूंगा।।

SHAHEEN ANSARI

She is pursuing Masters in Microbiology. And the one who try to put her thoughts in words of her imaginary world with her unique viewpoint. She is a free soul of an utopia with a perspective of protopia. Her viewpoint to see the world have always been come up as the hog heaven were everything is just perfect and fulfilled.

सलाम

आपको दोस्ती का सलाम लिखेंगे,
दिल की किताब में अपना अरमान लिखेंगे,
काश मिल जाए आसमान की हुकूमत,
सितारों की जगह आपका नाम लिखेंगे।
ना करते शिक़ायत ज़िन्दगी से कोई,
अगर मान जाता माना ने से कोई,
किसी को क्यों याद करता कोई,
अगर भूल जाता भुलाने से कोई।
ज़िन्दगी में हर बार ये मुकाम आए,
तुम हमारे हम तुम्हारे काम आए,
बस इतनी दुआ है खुदा से,
की हर जनम में तेरे दोस्तों में मेरा नाम आए।।

BOND BY HEART

By chance met the few folks and they turns out to be my Family. That family who holds me at my worst and always have their back in hard times. That family who makes any moment memorable by just their presence. The family who supports and accompany in every crazy streaks and be their for each other at any adverse state. Blessed to have you guys in my life and thank you for making my life more brighter and quintessence by your existence. They have always been there at any second for help and by giving back to each other that only makes our bond special. And especially the food is the one that connects us all like it is that string which keeps us joined. And the best thing that we hate the same people and do gossips and just do lame teenage girly things which every girl does in their school. They are my safe place where I can say anything and be the original me. And I know that I would be accepted like what and how and who am I.

KAREENA VERMA

She is kareena verma The Daughter of Mr.Kehru verma & Mrs.Rajeshwari verma . She is a computer science student and currently pursuing the bachelor of application And she is very passionate in writing and co- author of many anthologies and as well as many international Anthologies too. In this world only her pen & diary is the best friend to penned her pain in the blank pages of life Diary .

And same as her name Kareena delineate alike her name , sanguine with her soul, pure with her heart , innocent with her straightforward thoughtful perceptions!

For her Rectitude within her is everything & nothing is above than Viracity with our nation , she wants only to flame alike terracotta Diya, for one day she'll spread the happiness of lights as the most bright star in the sky of someone home and just wanna to spread love of humanity every where !!

LOVE VIBES

Whenever I meet you,
to talk with you I just lost myself forever in you,
Those 1 am talk with you ,
My silliness questions & your sweet answers,
Hehe ! How do I always bored you with it?
"Do you ever cry ?" ,
Yes as usual , always
"You said to me with shyness"
I always asking to myself ,
"How do we both feel to each other?"
Without saying any words
"How do we understand to each other with just text formats?"
I don't know , why those weird feelings happened with us ?
Sometimes I thought , I'm disturbing you,
"I don't wanna distrub you" with my words ,
I don't wanna hurt you ever with my words,
I don't wanna lose you ever,
to lost myself again And
"if someone ask to me" What did you get best ever in this year? "
I'll tell your name just only my friend"
Thankyou to being my soulmate of my every tearful pains !

WHY ARE YOU ALWAYS NICE WITH ME?

Why are you always nice with me?
Why do you make me so much special everyday with more care
of mine!
How do you feel my pain,
when I'm really not okay,
but I'm replying you in the text " that I'm fine ,
please don't worry at all"
Why I'm so Possessiveness about you
"Am I really fall in love with you?"
When you talk to me
When you share your favourite songs with me
And how is turn into my favourite too,
when I meet you in my dreams always;
When you hold my hands Kiss me on my forehead,
You came across to touch my neck,
When I'm really in Deep pain,
frustrated You just hold me in your shoulders,
How you hug me tightly,
than I forget everything in you,
please don't left me hold me tight in arms,
You came in my a blooming flower in winter,
Let's just listen our both fav song in headphones!
With one cup coffee with you !

NAVEEN BHARDWAJ

Myself Naveen Bhardwaj a programmer by profession a lover of poetry maker and like reading books and audiobooks and has telegram channel and wants to write in more anthologies in future if he gets a chance.

LATE NIGHTS

Give me your hurt,
I will wipe away your tears,
Give me your trust,
I will wipe away your fears,
Give me your love,
I will wipe away the years,
Show me your achy memories,
I will make them disappear,
Show me your dreams,
I will let out a cheer,
Show me your true color,
I will clean the smear.

KRISHNA MOTWANI

Krishna Motwani is a Student currently.
She use to pen down her feelings.
She is a moody girl.
She started writing in the month of june,2020.
She writes in her free time.
She writes some motivational quotes or poetries too and practices artworks also.
She lives her life like a bird
As bird flies freely and enjoys life like that she also lives her life freely and enjoy fullest.

OPEN LETTER TO BEST FRIEND (SISTER BY HEART)!

You are the one who changed my life from those dark shades of pain into a bright shine, the one who gives me hope in difficult situations, the one whom i share everything freely only and only because i trust you. You can't imagine that how much special you are! When we both met, that time we were just friends but now you are my everything like you are only my world! That our first meet was bit uncomfortable for me to talk to you and was bit scared that how would you react to my talks but now i use to share each and every moment with you even that incidents which i never share to my family! You are not my blood sister but you are like my soul sister. I just dont have words to express my feelings for you. You are my heaven. You came in my life to give happiness and smile on my face and removed all of darkness from my life. Whenever i talk to you, just a unique smile comes on my face. Remember that day of our childhood when our mothers didn't allowed us to talk to each other. And see now, we are not just friends , we are soul sisters. I just feel free to share things to you, it gives me relief, removes my stress! I wish, May this friendship will as like now till our last breath. Keep smiling my dear special one!

ZAINAB SABOOWALA

Zainab Saboowala is a dreamer and believer from Mumbai. She's a night lover and works on being a good human rather than great one. Her writings are her thoughts, emotions and feelings put into words. She believes when you can't say it, write it. She is optimistic and loves spreading smiles around.

Pen name - Zain

यारों का साथ

मिले थे हम उस सफर पे,

मंजिल के उस डगर पे,

एक अनजान सा चेहरा जो अपना बन गया,

पराया जो था,

ज़िन्दगी का वो एहेम हिस्सा बन गया,

खुशी में जिसके जश्न मनाएंगे,

गम में साथ आसू बहाएंगे,

भले रास्ते जुदा हो पर साथ कदम बढ़ाएंगे,

एक दूसरे का हौसला बन जाएंगे,

हाथ थामे साथ निभाएंगे,

ये ज़िंदगी ए यार तेरे नाम कर जाएंगे।।

मेरे यार

मैं तो अपने सपने पूरे करने निकली थी,

राह में मुझे साथी मिल गए,

बेगानो के बीच कुछ अपने मिल गए,

दोस्ती का हाथ थामे हम सफर पर चल दिए,

दोस्तो के लिए हमने,

अपने रास्ते बदल दिए,

खुद ने चोट खाई उनको दर्द तक ना होने दिया,

अपने सपनो के आगे,

दोस्तों को रख दिया,

चाहे ले लो इम्तेहान जितने,

हर मुश्किल में हम एक साथ है,

आँख मूंद कर जिसपर है यकीन साथी वो बेमिसाल है,

वो है तो सब कुछ है,

उनके बिना तो जीत भी हार है,

मेरे यार के बिना,

मेरा हाल बेहाल है,

खुद से भी ज़्यादा मुझे अपने यारों से प्यार है ।।

AMI PATEL

She is Ami Patel from Ankleshwar. 25 years old. She is writer, poet and book reviewer. She loves travelling. Her writing comes out of her feelings of her deepest relationships and its purity. She is also available on youtube to share her views and writing. She works in human resource department. She appreciates life with its all perspectives.

LET'S VISIT BEACH AGAIN

It had been a week and I knew that you were not in town. Where did you go without telling me? This was the first time you behaved like that. You didn't show up even on my birthday morning. Suddenly my grandparents, whom I had never seen, got out of your car, stretched out their arms, and called out to me in the evening. Dad was kicked out of the house after my mom and dad's love marriage. Dad himself never saw them after that. No one knows what you explained to them but you made up for the biggest shortcomings of my life. That's when I found out what you were hiding and why you were missing for those two or three days. I gave up all the hope of meeting my grandparents but you did not give up because you have got a big heart like the sea. Peaceful and soft. I can't express my happiness and gratitude in words but let's meet at the beach to feel my heartbeat once again..

HALF TRUTH

Twelve days after Nishant's death due to Corona, His wife Shavi, began to claim all of Nishant's property on her own name. They also had a girl. Every member of Nishant's house was shocked by her behavior. Shavi started living separately with his daughter. One day Nishant's parents came to Shavi's house remembering as they were missing their granddaughter very much. There they heard Shavi telling this to a man she was living with- "Our daughter called you 'Daddy' for the first time today. Eventually, she forgot about Nishant and recognized her true biological father. If I had not given drug to Nishant, We would have been separated for a few more years, but in the end we are together and rich. I told you that I will not let your poverty come between our love. The doctor also took our side on the name of Corona..."

MOHAMMAD SOHAIL

He is Mohammed sohail from Hyderabad and pursuing his bsc nutrition
And he also participated in many anthology books. He also write very good writer.
He likes to explore more by his write-ups.

SIMPLICITY

Simplicity makes a man perfect,
Never get cross to your attitude,
If you do that,
You will loose your identity

-MOHAMMED SOHAIL

GIFT

Mom and dad are best gift,
There are the life,
They are the world,
Never miss them,
Never leave them,
They are the life of everything....

-MOHAMMED SOHAIL

ESHA YADAV

Esha Yadav is 16 year old, She is from Greater Noida, blessed with acting and writing!

वक़्त गुजर गया

शुरुआत थी तो फूल खिला,

समझ आया,

अब मुरझाया क्यूं?

अब वक़्त नहीं,

समझ आया,

तो पहले झुठलाया क्यूं?

अधूरे पल!

हम फजूल के ही सही,

पर हमारा ज़क्रि तो कर,

प्यार ना सही,

पर हमे याद तो कर!

PANKAJ RAJPUT

He thinks, A creative message describing your unique selling,
Whether you think you can or you think you can't, you're right.
All he do is win, but no matter what.
Started writing recently but now is a co-author of some anthologies.

एक अजनबी रिश्ता

मिले जब हम तुमसे तो बन गए अफसाना,

सारे उन लम्हों को फिर से जिए तो बन गई यादें सारी,

कितने प्यारे थे वो दिन,जो साथ गुजारे,

जी चाहता हैं साथ तुम्हारे पूरे कर लूं दिल के अरमान सारे,

ना जाने कब एक अजनबी ने खुली आंखों से दिखा दिए नजारें।

दिल का रिश्ता

ये दिल का रिश्ता बड़ा अजीब है,

कभी हंसाता है,कभी रुलाता है,

तो कभी तन्हाई में भी यादें दे जाता है ।

ये दिल का रिश्ता बड़ा अजीब है,

कभी अपनों से भी टूट जाता है,

कभी गैरों से भी जुड़ जाता है,

गहरी सी इस नींद में मीठे सपने दे जाता है ।

ये दिल का रिश्ता बड़ा अजीब है,

बिना बात के मुस्काता है,

आंसू को भी अनमोल बना जाता है,

तेज़ धूप में भी छांव सी दे जाता है।।

AGAM SACHDEVA

She is an extremely talented girl with a very beautiful mind. She writes so well at such a young age. Though, she is just 14 years old but still is adored by many People. She has been a part of many anthologies earlier and made her parents proud. She is beautiful creation of God.

FRIENDSHIP

You came into my life as am unexpected gift,
And now from my life I would not let you drift.
As I sit down in the night sky,
I think of flying with you too high.
I love how special our bond is,
And we never please.
Our friendship means the world to me,
And I Love you that much,
that you can't even see.

BEST FRIEND

Best friends are somebody who stick together till the end,
They are like a straight line that never bends.
They are our true Love,
And living without them is quite tough If I am bread,
he is Nutella If I am the One in tears,
he is the umbrella,
It's a blessing that has stuck on me and with him,
I am always in glee.
Lastly, I Love him More than anybody.

M.HARSHINI

She is M.Harshini. She is 23years old. She is very well talented in writing, poetry and a short story in both Tamil and English. She has the talent to write poetry within 10 minutes after knowing the topic. She writes more and more in her life.

MY DEAR SISTER BY HEART

My dear lovely,
you are the affectionate person in my life.
with lots of concern on me sweetie,
with tons of love in my life,
which was shown by you.
A lot of happiness in our life ; where we spend together?
A lot of care in life ; To shine together,
In our fragrance of presences of life.
I forgot my sorrows, when I am with you?
To lead my tomorrow's, I love to leave with you,
To lead my whole life.
I am unable to come to your home,
To see you daily in my life.
I am waiting for our roam,
To enjoy the day of life,
Through our heartful affection.
I waited for our meeting,
To spend time with you,
But you came with your greeting,
To see you in marriage,
with your lovable companion,
I remember our golden days ; To reconnect our memories,
The day where we play which creates beautiful memories,
From the purest relationship in our life.
Oh my dear beauty you are not only beautiful through face,
Also, you are beautiful through your attitude,
And also through your character.

BEAUTY OF RELATIONSHIP

To lead your happy life,
Relation by heart is more beautiful,
Than the relation by blood,
Which gives tons of love to us.

AKASH CHAURASIYA

This is Akash Chaurasiya from Azamgarh living in Lucknow. He completed his intermediate from KV AMC Lucknow. He is a commerce student. He loves to write Hindi poems and English articles. He writes hilarious poems especially on the sad topic. He is love nature photography. He has participated in 15+anthologies.He want to travel world, meet new people, make them friends, want to know new culture of the society.

मेरा ये भाई

कोई हम अलग कैसे कर सकता है यहां,

खून से नहीं,

दोस्ती हमने दिल से की है,

सारे खेल संग खेले है,

संग मुसीबतें झेले है,

छोटी लड़ाइयां भी हमेशा हमने मिल के की है,

बचपन से ही तेरी सारी खूबी जानते है,

सबसे ज़्यादा प्यारा तुझे अपना मानते है,

कोई हमारे बीच दरार कैसे ला सकता है,

बचपन से ही,

दोस्ती की हदें सारी लांगते है,

दिल मेरे संग मेरे भाई के,

ये भाई रहता है,

मेरी मुसीबतों में मेरे संग ये भाई रहता है,

रिश्ता हमारा खून ना हो तो क्या हुआ,

साथ रहेंगे हम,

दिल छू लेने वाली ऐसी बात ये भाई कहता है।।

तृष्णा

उसको ये खबर नहीं कि वो मेरी जान है,

मेरे दिल में रहने वाली वो अकेली मेहमान है,

उम्र में बड़ी है मगर सबसे करीब है मेरे वो,

पाकर उसके जैसी कोई,

मुझे दोस्ती पे अभिमान है,

मेरी सभी गलतियां माफ़ करती है,

मुझसे वो मिलने का जाप करती है,

वो असम की मैं पूर्वांचल का लड़का,

मेरे खुशी मै शामिल,

दुख मे वलिाप करती है,

हमारा रिश्ता खून का नहीं दिल का है,

मेरे दिल के वो सबसे करीब रहती है,

बड़ी बहन का काम,

तृष्णा उसका नाम,

भूलू कैसे उसे,

खयालों में संग रहती है।।

TRISHNA CHAKRABORTY

Trishna Chakraborty is a writer from Haflong, Assam. She is a Student of English literature. She writes poetry, quotes and micro tales stories. She write about her thoughts and her feelings. She is a co-author of 25+ anthologies and a compiler. She wants to be a famous writer.

LETTER TO AKASH

Hi, My jan Akshu How are you? I hope you are super good. You know I meet you when i was feeling very low and lost in memories. But after meeting my life got changed. You know everyday and each moment is full of happiness because of you. I am really glad that you came in my life.we were on the group but never chat personally, one day I put a story on my insta and you replied that you want chocolate from me. I will never forget that and I want to give you many more chocolates my akshu. I remember the day it was New Year when I put a status that anyone who want to do a video call with me . I think this was the best status the first time we were on a video call, the best day ever.. My brother you are my love, my best friend. I am so lucky to have you. Always be happy and keep smiling I am there slwsysy.. I know you will be always there for me and I want to let you know that there is a surprise for you on your birthday I have planned..you will get it soon.. Lots of love to you my jaan Akshu.. Happy birthday to u..

Yours lovely sister Trishu

मेरे प्यारे भाई

मेरी जान हो तुम,

मेरा भाई हो तुम,

मिले ते किस्मत से,

पर दिल जुरा था,

पहले से तुझसे मिलने को दिल तरसे,

तू मेरी खुशी है,

मेरी जिंदगी भी,

आँखों में एक बूंद भी ना तू देख पाए,

इतना प्यारा सा हे तू,

ढेर सारा प्यार तुझे तू मेरी दुनिया,

मेरा प्यारा अक्षु हे तू,

नाम आकाश है तेरा मेरी मुस्कराहट है तू।।

KRISHAN KANT SEN

A local boy from Baran Rajasthan, Krishan Kant Sen is a passionate writer. Currently working on his debut novel. Professional primary teacher likes to work with glorious words. He completed his Master's Degree in English from Kota University. His write-ups published in various anthologies in English and Hindi both languages. Mostly works with stories,but sometimes he connects with poetry too. Frictional works is his main need. He loves to spend time with pen and paper. He loves to read novel of romance genre mostly.

MINE OR NOT MINE

Hey! My dear lovely Lifeline.
You're not mine, But you're mine.
I never expected such response from You.
I need my dead life just like you.
You have more secret in you.
I don't want to see, secret in You.
You're too far from me.
Some secret also hidden in me.
I want to talk you more.
I wish to listen you more.
You're not fine, when you're silent.
You looking fine, when You're violent.
You're like me in cadar of life.
I also do same everywhere in life.
Life seems to be similar.
I don't like to lose deliver.
You have to fight back again.
If you didn't get me, All in vain.

TWIN FROM ANOTHER MOTHER

Hey! My dear twin Anshika.
You're just like veronica.
Who fought back in every mild situation.
You are my sister by emotion.
I never see you to survive.
You inspired me for life derive.
You are my helping hand.
You helps me for love tend.
You support me forever.
My motives as like you deliver.
Its just virtual world, where we meet yet.
But never feels that, We didn't meet yet.
My last wish to celebrate birthday together.
Because You're my twin from another Mother.

SAIKUMAR ENDUNURI

He is Saikumar Edunuri belong to Telangana . Pursuing BSC. BZC at chaitanya institution and He is a writer of broken quotes and life quotes and writing quotes is his passion and wrote many quotes which are on his id called justin_sk_kings and here he is for writings quotes for any one who wanted on any topic...His motto is always to help change the world on every step.

REAL LOVE IS NOT IN BLOOD BUT IN HEART

Love of my wife is greater than love of my daughter bcoz my daughter loves me bcoz she is my blood but my wife loves me more than herself even though she is not my blood or anything but only bcoz she is my heart and am her heart beat forever until our soles get burned ---- BY ESK

LOVE THAT IS BORN FROM HEAT BUT NOT FROM BLOOD

I have many people those who are having same blood of mine in their body like my relatives , cousins etc but none of them made my heart to beat faster when I see them but the one whom I met somewhere in unexpected times and in the journey of my life is the one who makes this heart to moves some more milli inches in and out bcoz that heart has some magic which stole my heart and beats on this heart until we are alive ---- BY ESK

ARCHISHMAN SATPATHY

Archishman Satpathy,often called the Enthusiast. Writer is a young dynamic writer from Deogarh, Odisha. He is presently pursuing B.tech from IIIT Bhubaneshwar. He started writing Qoutes and short poetries from young age of 16 and had now made it as his passion. He has contributed as co-author in more than 180 anthologies. He is an author of the book*LAKEEREIN ZINDAGI

ROMANCE WILL WII

Was she aware of this mishap
The blame game can't be played
For luck be playing another role
Just a beginning of the Innings
And the story began again now
This time lot of agreements present
In the court with both as justice
They play the role of life and soul
The intense for each other was speechless
They are always the place of holy shrine
For both of them as each Valentine
They tried winning the battle and succeed
Their living was surprisingly regardless
The issues are therefore solved and
Minds filled with griefs of both are clean
Now for the world their hearts are locked
And their romance verse is scripted
Now their love is tested with all dark apart
And yes, their romance captured all and win

WARRIORS OF PANDEMIC: RELATION APART

A salute can't express the thanks
That I want to convey our warriors
A respect campaign is also ample
For those godly people who saved us In the fear of virus, they teached us
The importance and meaning of life
Their efforts should be scripted in books
They must get a chance to win awards
Their family love from all over the nation
They put forth our flag instead pandemic
Due to them we are living happily today
We love you so much all the covid warriors
Without you, we can't get the comeback
The soul is saluting you today by heart
Today the world is saluting your efforts

A.K. AGRAWAL

A. K. Agrawal is a young and upcoming writer from Chhattisgarh who is pursuing to become a doctor. He is very fond of writing and is a bright student. He has the talent to make people think about his poems again and again. He plays with words very interestingly that there are small and hidden meanings in his poems that only few can know what it means.

RELATION OF ME AND MY MOTHER

Me and my mother battling with a disease,
That is known as Erythroblastosis feotolsis...
This means my blood is different from my mom,
And every baby after the first will be dead after born...
But how great is this nature,
For the balance it provides some features...
The relation between a mother and baby is so strong ,
Even if it isn't connected with blood ,
still the love grows in the womb...
We both doesn't want each other to get hurt by our bodies ,
Even if the blood makes dangerous antibodies...
Technology too helped us ,
that strong is our relationship ,
We don't need the same blood but heart to live...
Different blood groups can't make me and my mother apart ,
Because our bonding is not of blood but of heart...
- A. K. Agrawal

FRIENDSHIP

I don't know how this will sound..
But I won't say it round and round...
My friend's connection with me is from heart...
With doesn't make us all hurt...
My blood relations always betrays me..
And I cry on my friend's shoulder and we are WE...
We aren't from no mean blood bound...
But we are so connected that each other's presence heals every
wound...
- A. K. Agrawal

ABDUL RAHMAN

He is Abdul Rahman S/O Abdul Ajij Khan from Banda Uttar Pradesh.His pen name is **रहमान बाँदवी** . He is a Mechanical engineer.

He is currently working as an assistant project engineer at Banda.He worked as a center manager,mission manager,examiner and trainer.

They are gonna keep people together. That's why they say........

First it reminds that Hindus, Muslims, Sikhs and Christiabs are brothers.

He is also an author of *चल कलम* and compiled anthology *कसिसा ए जहां*,

Curiosity and co author in many anthologies.

Writing is a good passion so writer by passion.

रिश्तों की महत्ता व ज़माने के साथ चलना

काफी समय पहले की बात है कि कई दोस्त मिलकर अध्ययन हेतु किसी एक शहर के एक विद्यालय में अपना पंजीकरण सुनिश्चित करा लेते हैं और साथ में रहकर पढ़ाई करते हैं परंतु ये तो जीवन है अर्थात पढ़ाई के अलावा दैनिक जीवन में भी तो व्यस्त होना ही पड़ता है इस तरह वो सभी अपने-अपने कामों में भी व्यस्त रहते । ये भी ज़ाहिर सी बात है कि सभी का अपना अपना मिजाज़ अर्थात स्वभाव अलग-अलग होंगे । इनमे से एक सीधा व सरल स्वभाव का था तथा व्यवहार भी सकुशल था परन्तु लोग उसके मिजाज का गलत उपयोग करते रहे फिर उसने संगति से कुछ न कुछ सीखने की कोशिश करता जा रहा था लेकिन फिर भी पूर्ण रूप से वो चालाकी न सीख सका । संस्थान के दोस्त व कुछ करीबी उसको इतना महत्व नहीं देते थे जितना की अन्य साथियों को दिया करते थे परंतु कुछ साथी महत्व देते भी थे तो कोई न कोई कारण से लेकिन वह इस बात को न समझता और खुश हुआ करता कि लोग उसे चाहते हैं । होता यूँ की जब भी कोई वित्तीय इत्यादि आवश्यक कार्य हेतु कुछ भी ज़रूरत हो तो उससे मांगते और इस तरह वो उनकी मदद करता रहता था और कुछ करीबी दोस्त,अहबाब आदि छोटा-छोटा करके कुछ धनराशि वसूल करते रहते लेकिन वापसी का जल्दी नाम न लेते जब वह टोकता तो एक जवाब मिलता कि यार लेके भाग थोड़ी न जाएँगे इस तरह समय बीतता गया और पढ़ाई पूरी करने के उपरांत अपने अपने गंतव्य की ओर चल पड़े पर लेनदेन का सिलसिला चलता रहा और लेते फिर वापस कर देते जिससे गाढ़ा विश्वाश कायम रहा लेकिन कुछ समय बाद पुराने व नए दोस्त बने पर उसकी आदत को

अच्छी या बुरी कहें ये समझ न आता कि वह अपनी नरमदिली के कारण सभी पर विश्वास जल्दी कर लेता परन्तु उसका रवैया वैसा ही रहा जिसका नाज़ायज़ फ़ायदा लोग उठाते इसी प्रकार फिर कुछ लोगों ने,व्यापारियों ने बड़ी धनराशि लेकर गायब गए । समय है कभी एक सा नहीं रहता और यही लाइन एक बार उस पर लागू हो गयी कि अचानक किसी कार्य हेतु कुछ धन की ज़रूरत पड़ी तब उसने अपने उन्हीं कुछ करीबियों, दोस्तों से धन के लिए आग्रह किया परन्तु सभी ने हाथ खड़े कर दिए । कहते है न कि अक्सर छोटी छोटी बातें घर कर जाती हैं इस प्रकार वह अक्सर चिंतित रहता कि आख़िर क्या खोया और क्या पाया । एक तरफ जहाँ उसकी ये सोच थी कि वह अपने स्तर अच्छे कार्य करके अक्सर सभी (दोस्त,रिश्तेदार आदि) को आपस में एकता और प्रेम में बाँधे रखेगा परन्तु वह इसमें विफिल हो गया । कहते हैं न कि इंसान गुण की अपेक्षा अवगुण को जल्दी प्राप्त करता है ठीक इसी प्रकार संगत में अपनी छाप तो न छोड़ पाया वरन कुछ अवगुणों को सीख लिया । इस प्रकार जरूरी नहीं कि ख़ूनी रिश्ते ही सीख दे कुछ व्यवहारी रिश्ते भी बहुत कुछ सिखा जाते हैं। कुछ व्यवहारी रिश्ते वास्तव में आपसे कुछ नहीं चाहते और उनके जीवन में आपकी आपके प्रति काफ़ी लगाव रहता है।

सीख:-

1. समय के अनुसार आप खुद को बदलो वरना समय तो बदल जाएगा और आप दरकिनार कर दिए जाओगे ।

2. कुछ व्यवहारी रिश्ते खूनी रिश्तों से भी ज़्यादा आपको महत्व देते हैं।

KOMAL CHAUHAN

Komal Chauhan is 19 years old. She is Pursuing Bachelor Of Business Administration. She is from Ranchi, Jharkhand. She loves writing and writes what she feels. It is her first book as co-author. She is into poetry.

THE REASON

Oh, I don't want this moment to pass I whispered in kuraid's ears. As we met after 5 years of long wait.We both were so in love at that moment. I am kashna. Kuraid is my first and forever. Kuraid has issues with his family so basically he lives alone. Sometimes I wonder how is it possible to love someone so much. And now I can't even think of living without him and he loves me the same way as I do. I feel the luckiest as I have him.You must be wondering how can any love story be so perfect. Even I used to think the same, till I found him cheating on me. Yes it's been 6 months since we broke up. He left me for another girl. I am still not over him and it is so obvious as it is not easy to forget 7 years relationship in 5 months. And my life changed after that. I detached myself from everything I used to love once. Beacause the one whom I loved the most left me. I was not in that state to feel anything I was numb.I used to work and only work just to keep myself busy. No socializing, nothing. I started disliking myself. I had my own anger issues, tantrums. I was hurt not only in my heart but in my whole body. Because heartbreak breaks you from inside. I was half dead. But there is a saying which says " let it hurt you and give birth to a new you". And same happened to me. Years passed. And now I am everything a person desires to be. I am the owner of' " Avians" (the trade Company) . And we are leading 2nd in the "Business Times". And my book " Positive sides of Heartbreak" has reached heights. I am self stable. And growing more and more.

So one fine day I was just on my way to my office a small kid walk towards my car saying didi, papa has not arrived yet to take me home. So I asked for his father's number and called him. His father came to take him. And I could not believe it is kuraid, yes he is married and the child was his son. I didn't uttered even a single word and walked away. As I don't want all that shit again.

Relations Par Coeur

Kuraid called me and said to meet up. When we met he said that he never cheated on me, he left me because that girl was a psycho who warned him that if he will not leave me, she will destroy my career as she was daughter of some ministrate.

It was hard to believe whatever he said but then I did.. And that girl lost her memory in a accident. And that child is not his son. He adopted him as he was alone. He said that he missed me every single day. And it was really tough for him. And I was in tears. I had everything in life still I was alone because Kuraid complete me. We both married and kept that child together. It is rightly said " whatever happens happens for a reason". I would not have been what I am today if Kuraud would have not broken me.

KAJOL GOLCHHA

Kajol Golchha is a English poet Writer. She is pursuing final year in

B.Tech biotechnology. She was born on 21st June 2000. She likes to write poems, quotes, blogs. She loves to read stories ,novels, poem. She used to spend time on seeking new things and she was very enthusiastic to learn everything.

ONE EVERLASTING NIGHT

The last night
You're in my arms
I'm in your lap
The moments where we
Smiled more and
Craved for each other.
I felt that my heart skips beating and
The entire universe stops
The first kiss which electrifies my body and
Made my heart to flutter faster.
When I looked into you
My eyes got sparkles with
A blush in my face
You took one step closer to me
I feel like my heart was locked
You came as key to open
My heart with ur magic of love.

CHERRY BLOSSOMS IN MY HEART

It's everywhere spring covered with beautiful cherry blossoms
It's been a decade still I remember about you
Where we are like cookies and cream
Everytime Im wandering with the memories
Which you left for me
They reminisce as a memory in my heart
Whenever cherry blooms I see you in
My heart with bursting tears.

BEENA SHAH

Beena Shah, is a homemaker from Gujarat. She is fond of writing poems, quotes and singing songs. She loves to write in four languages Gujarati, Marathi ,Hindi and English She has also co-authored 12+ anthologies. Check out her writings on her blog and on YourQuote

वो दिल ही क्या

वो दिल ही क्या जो धड़कना न जाने,

तुम्हारे साथ रहकर भी संभलना न जाने...!

ख़्वाबों के रास्ते का सफर

ये दिल से ही तो शुरू होता है ।

पर फिर भी यह कहीं तो रुक ही जाता है ।

वो दिल ही क्या जो ठहरना न जाने,

किसी एक राह पर रुकना न जाने ।

बार बार टूटता है यह,

फिर भी जुड़ता है यह ।

कोई आस ऐसी जो उसे दिलासा देती है,

हमेशा एक नई ख़्वाहिशों से भर देती है ।

ये दिल ही क्या जो सपने ना दिखाए,

और पूरे होते ही मचलना न जाने।

वो दिल ही क्या जो संभलना न जाने,

वो दिल ही क्या जो धड़कना ना जाने।।

सज़ा - ए - प्यार

बस एक नजर प्यार भरी

हो गई मैं बांवरी ।

सपनों में खोई पल पल ,

मदहोशी सी छाई हर पल ।

नजर का चला ऐसा जादू,

दिल होता रहा बेकाबू ।

दस्तकों की आहट से परेशान मेरा मन ,

वक्त बेवक्त महसूस करें

एक अजीब सी घुटन ।

मुझे यूं सताने वाले ,

हल्के से मुस्कुराने वाले ।

ठहर जाओ थोड़ा ,

जल्दी ही मिलेगी ,

तुम्हें भी ये प्यारी सजा ।

जब मैं करूंगी तुम्हें परेशान,

मत होना तुम हैरान।।

JAY KAILASH VYASS

He is Jay Kailash Vyass, 23years.Got to know about his skills in his second year of college and now he is in love with his this skills.

वादे तो हजारों थे तेरे मेरे दरमियान

वादे तो हजारों थे तेरे मेरे दरमियान .....

इरादे बडे नेक थे तेरे मेरे दरमियान .....

यादे तो वही है तेरे मेरे दरमियान .....

में तो वहीं हू पर अब तू नहीं है हमारे दरमियान .....

अब तो बस तेरी बहुत सी यादे और तेरे बहुत से वादे रह गए है पर सरि़फ

और सरि़फ मेरे दरमियान ...... वादे तो हजारों थे तेरे मेरे दरमियान .....

- जय कैलाश व्यास

ऐ साथी आज तुझसे मिलने का जी कयिा

ऐ साथी आज तुझसे मिलने का जी कयिा ......

तुझसे गले लग रोने का बहुत जी कयिा....

तेरी यादो में डुबे रहने का जी कयिा...

तेरे साथ कि गई लंबी लंबी बातें फरि देहाराने का जी कयिा...

साथ बैठ के चाय पीने का जी कयिा .....

इस पूरे समय को रोक कर फरि उन यादों में खो जाने का जी कयिा ......

ऐ साथी आज तुझसे मिलने का जी कयिा ......

तुझसे गले लग रोने का बहुत जी कयिा....

- जय कैलाश व्यास

RICHA SAINI

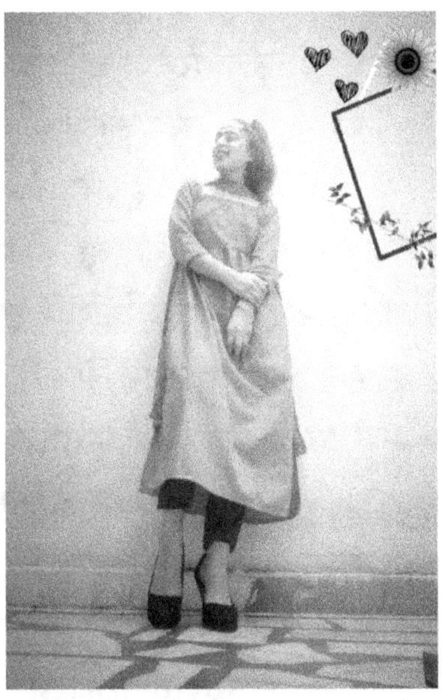

Richa Saini is pursuing Fashion Designing. She start writing when she was 15years old. She like to pen down her thoughts.

इंतजार करते

इंतजार करते आखिरी सांसो तक,

लौट आउगा,

एक बार कह कर चले जाते,

आज़ तक ज़ालिम निगाहें तुझे देखने को तरसती है,

एक बार करीब से इन निगाहों मे डूब कर चले जाते,

मोहब्बत है हमारी तुमसे जो कभी खत्म ना होगी,

एक बार अपने दिल की धुन सुना कर चले जाते,

इंतजार करते आखिरी सांसो तक,

लौट आउगा,

एक बार कह कर चले जाते,

विस्वास तो है तुझ पर,

भरोसा नहीं कमबख़्त दुनिया पर,

एक बार मुझे अपना बना कर चले जाते,

दुनिया ये बेशक बेगानी है,

तुम मेरे अपने हो,

ये दुनिया को जता कर चले जाते,

अब कहाँ ढून्दू तुझे मै,

अपना पता बता कर चले जाते,

छोड़ गए हों मुझे इस दुनिया मे,

इंतजार करूंगा तेरा उस दुनिया मे,

मुझे कह कर चले जाते,

एक बार बताया होता, हमारी गलती क्या है,

माफी मांगने के लिए,

तेरे पीछे उस दुनिया मे चले जाते,

या खुदा से भीख मांग कर तुझे वापसि इस दुनिया मे ले आते,

छोड़ गए हों बेशक छोड़ कर मुझे इस दुनिया मे मरने के लिए,

मेरा दलि तो मुझे वापसि कर के चले जाते,

जीती रहूं मै,

भरती रहूं साँसे इस काबलि तो मुझे छोड़ कर चले जाते,

इंतजार करते आखिरी सांसो तक, लौट आउगा,

एक बार कह कर चले जाते,

खुदा से आरज़ू करुँगी,

कि सीखा दे तुझे जब तक आऊ मै तेरे पास तेरी दुनिया में,

कि मोहब्बत करने वाले कभी छोड़ कर नहीं जाते।।

-रचिा

दो पल

जीके जदिगी देख ली ग़मों मे,

जीके जदिगी देख ली आंसुओ से,

जीके जदिगी देख ली ईमानदारी से,

जीके जदिगी देख ली वफ़ाई से,

बहुत सह लयिा दुनयिा का डर,

बहुत रूठ लएि हम खुद से,

बहुत कर लयिा भरोसा दूसरों पर,

बहुत जी ली जदिगी, टूटे दलि से,

ऐ मोला! मुझे 100 साल जदिगी नहीं चाहिए,

जदिगी देदे बेशक दो पल की,

पर वो दो पल जी सकूँ मै खुशी से,

वो दो पल जी सकूँ मै हँसी से,

जों 100 साल मे ना कर सकूँ वो कर सकूँ दो पल मे,

दूसरों की जदिगी भर दु खुशयिो से,

उन दो पलों मे,

हे! मोला दो पल जदिगी दे,

जनिहे जी सकूँ मै सकून से।।

-रचा

PRAGYA VERMA

Pragya Verma hails from Prayagraj, Uttar Pradesh. She is a poetess and a writer. She has done 115+ anthologies, and five international anthologies and six world record anthologies as a co-author. She is also compiling two anthologies named, "Shades Of Night", "In A Relationship With Success". She has a great interest in making paintings and doing photography. She loves to gain spiritual knowledge and tries to find peace everywhere.

SPECIAL BOND

In my life's darkest sky,
She's the moon who brings light,
There for me whether it's day or night.
Her friendship is like a rainbow in my dark sky,
Makes my heart happy and set me free to fly.
A special bond we share together,
I know that you'll stay with me forever.
Never let me fall apart,
She has a special place in my heart.
Many friends came and gone,
But, she's there in my darkest storm.
I know our relation is not by blood,
But, we are connected by our hearts.
We cried and laughed together,
She's my best friend forever and ever.

DHAIRYA MANOJ THAKKAR

Dhairya Thakkar is a 17 years old lad who scored 91.80% in SSC Exam. He is also a Rapper, Writer, Table Player and A Prodcast Host.

TRUE LOVE

Mahesh who completed his Graduation, proposed his college friend Ananya. Even Ananya liked him. They both loved each other but their relationship had a small obstacle. Mahesh had to go toh USA from India for 3 years for further studies. Couple's parents decided that Mahesh & Ananya will get married once Mahesh will come back after studies. For next 2 years, when Mahesh had gone to USA, Mahesh and Ananya were on contact via Instagram & calls. One day, Ananya had met an accident. Her Pharyngeal region got hurt and she lost her voice. Doctors said that she won't be able to now. Ananya was upset due to such an unexpected incident. She loved Mahesh and taught that this will ruin her as well as Mahesh's life. So, she decided to give up on this relationship. She wrote a letter to Mahesh saying that she don't wanna countinue this relationship. she asked Mahesh not to contact her. Mahesh didn't had any idea what happened. He tried to call her but all in vain. Ananya didn't reply him. After around 10 months, Mahesh visited Ananya's house when he knew her parents were out. He knocked the door, kept a letter there, and hid behind a tree. When Ananya came out, she picked up that letter. It read "Mahesh Weds Ananya". When she saw up, she noticed that Mahesh was standing in front of her. Mahesh (In sign language) said, "Hi My Love. How are you ? I came to know about your accident from your best friend. I tried to contact you to tell yu something but you didn't respond. Do you know that it took me 6 months to learn this sign language. I know that you can hear but I wanted to talk to you in your language. Just want to tell you that I Love You Ananya. When I proposed you, I told you that I will stay forever and I am keeping my promise. Would you Marry me by keeping your promise ▢. " Ananya was in tears...

Relations Par Coeur

Moral

1) Don't make Assumptions in Relationships.

2) If you can't keep your promises, then don't make any.

3) It is rightly said that "**वह पल सबसे प्यारा है, जब किसी इंसान ने किसी को प्यार करने में समय बतिाया है** I" And this is an example of this line 🕐

PARTH GALIA

Parth Galia is a 16 years old lad.He is a passionate writer, Researcher, Co-Compiler, Book Reader and Commerce student.

RELATION BY HEART, NOT BY BLOOD...

There's a small difference between Having a Relation and Keeping a Relation. People usually have relations just for personal benifit or just as compulsion. Instead, one should leran to make relation by Heart. It's right said by someone, "If you want to make this world a beautiful place to live, then become a Beautiful Person at First Place." Learn to help others without thinking about your benifit. If you want service, people may not serve you but if you want to serve others, who can stop you ? If you want help, people may not help you but if you want to offer help, who can stop you ? If you want everyone to become peaceful, people may not obey you but you want to be a peaceful individual, who can stop you ? Answer of all these questions is "No One" & by becoming a good person, by helping others & and being peaceful, whi can become a great individual and also, a people's magnet.

VANSHIKA PARMAR

Vanshika Parmar from Delhi. She is a student of class 12th driving on a road of writing.In writings her main focus goes on poems,Qoutes and sometimes macrotales.She write in both languages.But what she write is from the input of her overthinking and feelings of her everything happening around her which results input a beautiful output.So would love to go on with writing till the time her mind stops working forever and hearts get tired off from beating.It would be great to get herself engaged in deep with this road in order to get the chance of knowing people more and their lifestyles which can help her in thinking more and more.

AN UNTOLD STORY

2 were in love with each other
2 people of different religions were planning to live together
But they forgot the religious issues around them
The society issues around them
The story they wanted to create ,
Got stucked and was stopped in the middle
Both the girls despite being the society and their religion not
ready to accept them
Still were ready to accept each other
They were in love with each other
But their love was brutally killed
One got fired and other suicided
No one cared for them
They saw them as a disaster
Were burdened to not share their story with anyone
But their unbreakable love never got killed
The love was in the souls not in their body
Souls did meet each other after life
But in the society their story became an UNTOLD STORY
The one out of many more

BONDING BY HEART NOT BY THE BLOOD

In a world of strangers
Two eyes met
Two different lips curved in a smile to each other
From smiling it went off to daily Chit-chats
From strangers they became Friends
From being Formal to each other they turn to being Informal
They took a road which was different yet interesting
From talking few minutes ,
they turned to not resisting themselves from not taking with
each other
From real names ,
they kept Nicknames of each other
From sitting behind each other ,
they started sitting with each other ..
From no kind of concern they started concerning each other
From normal outing they used to have Nightouts
From having normal talks they shared each other's deepest
secrets
From knowing each other's favorite color to Choosing clothes for
each other From having an unknown relation to the deepest
relation
They never left each other in any situation..
From sharing no kind of bonf they turned to a special bond ..
BOND BY HEART .. which says NO DEMANDS, NO PAYBACKS
From school talks to college talks and to married talks ..
Their relationship never took break
As the road they took earlier made them come to an end with an
epic relationship..
And this relation was not by BLOOD

This relation was by HEART BOND OF BLOOD ISN'T ALWAYS BE WITH YOU SOMETIMES BOND BY HEART MAKES AN EPIC STORY WITH YOU

BANDITA SAHU

Bandita - She is a perfect ambivert, from Temple City - Bhubaneswar. Loves to travel and have adventures. To an unknown she might be a shy person, but she is really an open book. Her passion of reading books of different genres had always encouraged her to write. To her, writing is just like filling the paper with breathings of one's heart.

CONNECTED BY HEART

I don't know the name of relation, We share..
You are the soul,
Without which, my body is bare..
You get hurt, I get pain..
You are the pleasure,
Which I get from rain..
You smile, I get peace..
You are bread, I'm cheese..

ME AND YOU

Distance never mattered in our case,
Because you are close to my heart, in every phase..
Your voice, give me peace, I love you to tease..
You give me sparkle, due to which I shine,
I love you to call mine..

ANUBHAV JHA

An 18 year old ambitious ambivert.

Just trying to express his feelings in poetic forms, his thoughts are not tied by social norms.

He's eager to create some difference in the world through his writing skills.

He's a zealous learner in this plethoric field of writing.

He believes the world to be a matrix & himself to be a glitch in the matrix.

BROTHERS IN ARMS

Brothers in arms that's what we are,
I recollect we've met in the war of Qatar.
Not relatives by blood,
but our heart pounds together.
Since then our friendship bud,
with a promise of forever.
Brothers in arms that's what we are,
I recollect when together we smoked cigar.
We are soldiers,
with each count of our breath,
a warrior's spirit within us in life, till death.
Brothers in arms that's what we are,
sharing the days & stars with our wounds & scars.
We are sibling creed,
as a unit together we bleed.
Brothers in arms that's what we are,
too close in the war but still afar.
I remember you took a shot saving my life,
I remember how I took out the bullet of your chest with a knife.
Brothers in arms that's what we are,
writing this memoir am weeping through core,
I know you aren't here to listen to me anymore,
but still, you will, reside in these rhymes even after the war.

SELFLESS LOVE

Love Is An Emotion
You Gotta Feel It
You Maybe A Big Mess
That You Gotta Deal With
Love Ain't More Or Less
It's Just Selfless
When You Adore Someone More
Than Your Own
That's The Selfless Love
You've Shown No Desire, No Expectations,
Want Of Nothing Makes Your Love Stronger
Than Anything I Know
It Hurts Sometimes But You Just Like
Tasting These Bitter Sour Limes
When You Love Unconditionally
But Get Nothing Back
You Know You Won't Get Jill
But You Gotta Be The Jack.

PRERNA VERMA

She is writer who stumbles and learns and writes. She believes that experience equals more than thought.

नभिते रिश्ते

नसीब नसीब की बात है जनाब,

दिल का रिश्ता हो या खून का,

नभिाते तो हम दोनों को हैं,

बात बस इतनी सी है!,

दिल का रिश्ता खुद ने बनाया है,

और खून का रिश्ता खुदा ने बनाया है।।

वक़्त वक़्त की बात है

लोग कहते हैं..
सारे अपने तो हैं साथ,
तेरे फिर किसिकी कमी है तुझे,
हां माना! सारे अपने हैं साथ मेरे,
पर दिल का क्या?
वो नहीं मानता,
जब तक वो ख़ास शख़्स ना हो साथ मेरे,
जिसे मैंने दिल से अपना माना है।
कुछ पल ऐसा भी आता है,
जब सारे खून के रिश्ते एक तरफ़,
और वही दिल के रिश्ते एक तरफ़,
"कभी कभी खून के रिश्ते, दिल के रिश्तो के सामने फर्किं पड़ जाते हैं।"

MOHANAPRIYA.K

Co-author Mohanapriya.K is a good writer from Tamilnadu, India. She has completed her Bechelor degree in Engineering stream. She has been a writer for one year as her passion.She wants to be a best compiler and curator in future. She will try to express what comes to her mind through her words as it is. For her writing is a great art. Yet she sincerely hope that this writing journey of her will continue as sweetly as it is now and will bring many successes. She also loves singing, gardening and drawing.

OH! MY LOVE!

My dear love!
"Your love is like an addiction to me,
Because I could not be myself
for even a second without thinking about you,
You know the reason!
Waiting for you is always a pleasure for me,
I too am as thin as the wind,
My dreams are filled all around me as the air is spread
everywhere,
I will float in the air and fly everywhere through my dreams
about you,
For you I am waiting with many dreams in me,
You are with me, I am with you,
Our love with us, I will see heaven in this world,
And I will enjoy living in it with you,
Forever and ever.
Be with me always for me.
I am not without your love. "
By, Your love

TO MY SOULMATE!

The day to give a rose to a beautiful rose that looks like a rose.
After giving the rose to that rose she is beautiful! No.
That rose she gave me by hand is beautiful!
The suspicion is that the writing does.
In the heart of a beautiful dream that life will smell like the
beautiful scent of a rose if we get this rose as our life partner.
Heart and flower day like a beautiful blooming rose in hand.
She is just as beautiful as the beautiful colour of the rose!
A beautiful mole on her face,
like a snowdrop sitting on a rose.
My life was full of colors the day I thought my life would be
colorful if you came into my life.
Today we celebrate proposal day to fill those colors in your life
and in our lives. My heart blooms with a smile as I count you as
my angel who came to color my life.
I thought of many ways to propose how.
Many new ideas were stuck.
One of them is to write and propose a poem for you.
Every word in my poem is from my heart for you.
All the words thus shed have blossomed into poems on paper.

DANIYA NADEEM

Daniya Nadeem is a young writer and a dreamer.She firmly believes in writing with gratitude,and convey the feelings of her heart.For her,poetry is not just a way to express,but also a way to dive into the world of fiction,to travel into one's imagination and build on from there.She always try to rectify her flaws with words that her pen orders her to write.

GIVE HIM A MESSAGE OF ME

Give him a message of me
That these moments of adhesion
and madness do not stay forever,
Even centuries get passed over
and never lay forever.
Give him a message of me
that neither moon lies here
nor the moonlight
and the life has become weird.
For whom am I staying
These tracks remain querying.
Give him a message of me
That if ever his heart gets cumber
then he must weep a bit,
And after flowing some tears away
He must sleep with comfort.
Give him a message of me
that nothing is perfect.
Except the sole ALLAH and only with Him,
we associate hope!

I AM SEEKING

Being goomy this evening, once again
I'm in search of hues
Here is lying a jet darkness
I'm in search of fireflies
Sadness is prevailing everywhere with its unlatched hair
I'm in search of thirsts
All these stars have got tangled
I'm in search of circulation
A crowd is proceeding constantly
I'm in search of mates
Wished to seek the destination have lost
I'm in search of paths
All glees are irked of me
I'm in search of true life!
-Penned by Daniya Nadeem

JASMINE PANDA

Miss Jasmine Panda is presently pursuing M.Sc. Chemistry from Berhampur University, Odisha, India. She is a Gold Medalist and University Topper in her B.Sc. She is also continuing an internship CSIR-SRTP in IICT Hyderabad. She holds the post of Senate Member of the University for the session 2019-20 in Academic Pursuits. She is a Governor Awardee for YRC. She has received All-Rounder Award in her 12th standard for excellence in extracurricular activities along with studies. She has been Literary and Cultural Champion in her college days. Apart from being a versatile orator and debator, she has been a part of 230+ anthologies till now and loves to pen down her feelings! She is an amiable person interested in both Science and Literature, having a wide variety of interests like painting, sketching, acting, anchoring, debating, rangoli making, taking part in extempore, elocution and many more...

REMEMBER

Remember!
Do you remember the Chocolates we shared together?
Remember the moments we fought together?
Remember the mischiefs we hide together?
Remember the days we spent together?
The wonderful excuses for not doing homework,
The sleepy and tired faces made in the morning!
The dreamy imaginations in the last bench,
The weird ideas for bunking classes together!
The unforgettable memories in the school bus,
The fantasies that seriously have no end!
The notorious activities in the playground,
The playful naughtiness day in and day out!
The excited we become during sports time,
The lazy n' lethargic we feel in assembly time!
The strategic plans made to obscure from father,
The unsuccessful methods to hide from mother!
Do you remember the days we spent together?
Do you really miss the days we spent together?
-By Jasmine Panda

GANESH PATIL

This is Ganesh Sadashiv Patil. He is student of UG in field of Pharmacy. He has writer and poet, who writes 100+poetry in Hindi and Marathi language. He loves to write on love, humanity, motivation and social themes. He loves to write down his feelings, his thoughts on various topics which makes him a writer of one own kind.

प्यार की यादे

ए रात मेरे दिल में तू आ याद मुझको उसकी तू देती जा,

मिले थे हम जीस दिन उस दिन की याद मुझे तू देती जा,

प्यार कयिा था जीससे मैने उसकी खुशबू तू फैहलाती जा,

उसकी चेहरे की रौनको को तू मेरे इन नैनो में यु बसाती जा,

राह पर जीस चल पडे थे हम उस राह को तु भी बताती जा,

मंजिल जो तय की थी साथ हमने उस जीतकी खुशी देती जा,

वो थी खयालो में बसी मेरे उन खयालो को ताजा करती जा,

सपने जो मैने देखे थे उसके उन सपनो की बाते तू करती जा,

हसी उसकी जो होती थी चेहरे पर ऐसी हसी तू दिखाती जा,

रूपको उसके जो निहारता हूं उस रूप को दिल में बसाती जा।।

तुमनें ना जाना

याद मुझे तुम्हारी युं हे सताती रात को ना वो कभी सोने हे देती,

इस तरह हं तिडपता हूँ तुम बिनि में हाल हे मेरा तुम क्या जाणो,

वो मुख पे रेहनेवाली हसी तुम्हारी मुझे यूही प्यार में थी डालती,

अब उस हसी बिनि में हूं जिता कैसे हाल हे मेरा तुम क्या जाणो,

तुम होती तो युं खोया में रेहता तेरी खुशबू में सदा मेहकता रेहता,

आज भी वो दिनि करता हूँ याद में हाल हे मेरा तुम क्या जाणो,

बारीशो में हमारा युं हं भिगिना थंडी रातों में एकसाथ में जागना,

अकेला होता हूँ अब यहां तुम बिनि में हाल हे मेरा तुम क्या जाणो,

कब आवोगी तुम फिरि लौट यहां जिनि के लिये फिरि वो दिनि यहां,

अब सब ये सुना लगता हे मुझे यहां हाल हे मेरा तुम क्या जाणो।।

SHUBHAM RATHORE (री$HU)

A boy who is passionate about writing and side by side he does his job.
He wants to make his career in writing as an author.
A nice person with alots of skills of writing.

हाँ शायद मुझे प्यार हो रहा था

खुली आसमां में घुटन होने लगा है,

बर्फ में भी जलन होने लगा है ।

ऐसा कभी हुआ नही ये पहली दफा है,

खुद से ज़्यादा गैर पे ऐतबार हो रहा है ।।

हाँ शायद मुझे प्यार हो रहा है

नींदों में तेरा ही ख़्याब आने लगा है,

यादे तेरी हर घड़ी सताने लगा है ।

इतना दर्द है फिर भी ये कैसा मज़ा है,

बेसब्री से किसी का इंतज़ार हो रहा है ।।

हाँ शायद मुझे प्यार हो रहा है

तुझे खोने का ख़्याब डराने लगा है,

परछाई बन कर पीछे आने लगा है।

हर तरफ तूही नजर आये ये कैसा नशा है,

आँखें बंद करते ही तेरा दीदार हो रहा है ।।

हाँ शायद मुझे प्यार हो रहा है

दिल मेरा था अब तेरा होने लगा है,

दिमाक तेरे ख़्यालो में खोने लगा है।

मेरा मुझमे काबू न रहा ये कैसा वफ़ा है,

तुझमें समाने को रूह भी तैयार हो रहा है ।।

हाँ शायद मुझे प्यार हो रहा है

बगैर तेरे मेरे आँखें,रोने लगा है,

मेरा चैन और करार खोने लगा है।

अब खुद में ही न रहा ये कैसा सज़ा है,
मेरे जिश्म और रूह में दरार हो रहा है ।।
हाँ शायद मुझे प्यार हो रहा है
-री$hu..

मैं बीमार हूँ

पता नही क्या हुआ है मुझे,

जान जैसे जा रही है

जब जब साँसे ले रहा हूँ,

गर्म हवाएं समा रही है ।

जीने की कोशिश करू तो,

ये ज़िन्दगी डरा रही है

गम ज़िन्दगी में कम नही,

ऊपर से तेरी यादे सता रही हैं ।।

इश्क़ हुआ तो लगता है,

जैसे मौत पे मैं सवार हूँ

मैं बीमार हूँ, इश्क़ का शिकार हूँ ।।

भूख भी नही न लगती प्यास है,

न मिटती तेरी याद है

न नींद आती न ख़्वाब है,

जैसे आमावस्या की रात है ।

आखों से आँसू बहती है,

और तेरी यादों की बरसात है

आखों को तेरा दीदार तक नही,

न होता कोई बात है ।।

एक तेरी ही खातरि मैं,

मरने को भी तैयार हूँ मैं बीमार हु,

इश्क़ का शिकार हूँ ।।

जस्मि में निशान नही,

मगर जख़्म सनि में हजार है

इतना गहरा जो कयिा,

तुमने आँखों से दलि पे वॉर है ।

न दावा काम आती है,

न दुआ का मुझपे असर है

ये कैसा रोग दयिा तुमने,

तुझे पाने का जुनून सवार है ।।

हालत अब मेरी नाजुक है,

मैं आया तेरे दरबार हूँ

मैं बीमार हु ,इश्क़ का शकिार हूँ ।।

-री$hu..

RADHIKA SHARMA

She is Radhika Sharma from Delhi she believes pen is precious thing to write effective answers and poetry. She is an most talented girl with a very beautiful mind. She writes so well at such a young age. Many poetry events she will participate she will miss lots of anthologies because it was paid and i will love to participate in this anthology first time Though, she is just 21 years old but still is adored by many people. She has been a part of many ngo earlier and has made her parents proud. She is a beautiful creation of God.Thanks you all. To give us great chance.

Dedicated to Tabla Maestro Shri Ramesh Bhatt Sir (Ajrada Gharana- Vadodara city, India) (Died - 05/01/2021)

Sir you have died a legend,
In your own way,
In your own time,
And in your own era.
We will miss your tabla in Vadodara samiti,
The atmosphere you used to create,
That humbleness,
And that happy face.
I know you won't be able to read this poem,
But as a fan and student,
We really wish,
That you could have lived many more years.
We have seen you doing selfless seva,
Praying to Deva (God),
You always spread love to all,
But sorry to hear the sad call.
Due to corona all have gone here and there,
But thanks to social media apps,
That we know who is alive,
And who is dead.
Your hands on tabla were just magical,
A maestro in your own way,
You attracted others towards tabla too,
But sadly you left us incomplete.
From playing on stages,
To playing for God,
You always proved,
That you are unique in our way.

Relations Par Coeur

Not only the tabla family and Sai samiti family,
But those who don't even know you,
Would like to send you their gratitude and respect for you,
Because more than a tabla player that's the love you have
earned Sir.
May you rest in peace!
Thank you!

HIDDEN DEMOISELLE

She is known by her pen name HIDDEN DEMOISELLE. She wants the world to know her by her words. She is a WALLFLOWER. She dwells in a mystical world created by her own imagination.

LOVE THAT BLOOMS INDIGO!

If you are blue,
I'm violet
If you're water,
I'm the isle
Together we gave rise to a plant
A bright, delicate sapling of our mystical love
We grew it with our heart and own hands
It wasn't red like a rose or white like a dove
Because we're blue and violet on this land
Our love bloomed with fragrance of your shirt
Flourished within our hearts with fragrance of my skirt
Then again, it grew steadily, vigilantly with a perfect glow
Mixture of you and I, this plant flowered with hue of indigo

VOLUME OF SILENCE

By the river bank,
I'd see this guy Adorable!
He'd keep looking at sky
Never saw him hang around
Never did I even hear his sound
Silence was his home, his life
Just sitting by his side, all time
He'd look at me and smile
Wonderful human!
Peaceful and quiet
Our relation was undefined
Not friends, not lovers, hearts entwined
Pure soul he was, he just couldn't talk
Fingers entangled, miles we'd walk
Language of silence, language of signs
Forever I became his, and he became mine

KHUSHI ARORA

Khushi Arora is a student. Born and brought up in Delhi. She is a photographer, graphic designer, poet, writer, guitarist, and wants to be a psychologist in future. She loves to explore, trying her hands onto different feilds.she loves food, travelling and keen to learn new sports, languages and musical instruments. Growing up she started expressing her thoughts, opinions, experiences, imaginations and questions in her writings ,which is more like a theraphy to her.

POWERLESS TO ESCAPE

I have lost myself
In a storm of what if's,
In hovering over wishes and wants,
In balancing between like and love ,
In people fading from life,
In cherishing memories,
In finding irrational possibilities,
In unrealistic realities ,
In fantasized dreams,
In fictionalized imaginations,
In regrets of the past,
In Expectations of the next moment.
In figuring out my desires and needs ,
In making non-existing choices,
In pleasing others
Often at at he cost of my comfort
In filling voids ,
In building bridges,
In understanding silences,
In fascination of happy endings,
Making sense out of meaningless pauses .
Now powerless to escape
The prison of my mind

AND I MEET MYSELF

When reality turns scary,
I want earth to dig up
A deep hole and I ask
To please Consume me whole .
When i fear living ,
I prefer writing
Stories
Complete or incomplete
And breathe in them .
Because that's what
I can control
When world turns
Colder,
My pen weave letters
Like warm quilt
Of quality yarn
And i cover my fears ,
Under.
When i feel
Less of the world ,
I become lost
In world of words ,
And hide behind
TWENTY-SIX
ALPHABETS
When i feel leftout ,
I turn to
Empty pages
And i meet myself ....

DIKSHA MOTWANI

Diksha Motwani is a passionate girl from Mumbai, Maharashtra. She loves to pen her feelings. She is introvert but her pen makes her extrovert. She is a writer, singer, artist and a poet!

CAN I?

I really dont know,
What this wierd feeling is for,
I just wanna hug you tight,
And cry out all whats inside,
Just wanna have your shoulder,
To make me relief,
I just really dont know why am feeling lone and low,
Can you please be here for me?
Can I please cry?
Can I hug you?
-Diksha Motwani

ALFIYA SUROOR KHAN

She is doing her 12th from Indo Asian college, Bangalore. And also working for national service scheme. She writes when her feelings hit deep, When she can't bear the pain, or even out of pleasure and happiness. She pen downs what she feels and what she thinks.

MY FAMILY

We rarely meet,
We hardly talk.
Yes , we are not
Together by blood.
But by love ,
Affection, respect
And undefined attraction
That is only felt by heart.
No no you are wrong,
We are not just friends,
But a family forever

AGARSANA T K

Agarsana T K is pursuing her post graduation. She is fond of writing and reading..

Relations Par Coeur

On the birthday of most adorable and generous human Mahatmaji 2019, at fall of dusk, while get back towards the home after spending a memorable day with my dear souls, I was accompanied with one of my beloved souls, without realising the crowd started to blabber the senseless aspects with her in the rocket of road transport (private bus), full of stars one old moon with the similar appearance of the birthday soul like wearing spectacles, white dhoti and also holding a supporting stick started to converse with us. I was weird that why he was interrupting my blabber. He asked about our academics and I stated that I am doing UG in literature and she is working as Assistant Professor. Suddenly with excitement he said that it was great pleasure to merge us with literature. Times gone together we three left the travel. We both moved to the opposite direction of the old man to give some spicy treat for our tummy. Inspite of considering his old age he get back towards us and asked to keep a note and pen beside us while sleeping. At first I am not get the point why he was stating like that, within few seconds he replied for my confused expression, that the amazing intellectual of human beings were come out while sleeping. To preserve the most precious thoughts we need to note it (kannu)dear. With a evergreen smile he blessed and took a good bye from us.